KU-022-561

OLYMPIA

DEADLY TARGET

SHOO RAYNER

ORCHARD

ROTHERHAM LIBRARY SERVICE	
B518873	
Bertrams	28/10/2011
JF	£8.99
CLS	

In the year 776 BC, the first
Olympic Games were held in a town
called Olympia in Ancient Greece.
Many years later, a boy named Olly
grew up there, dreaming of being
an Olympic champion. But first,
he would have to be better than his
arch-enemy, Spiro...

ORCHARD BOOKS
338 Euston Road, London NW1 3BH
Orchard Books Australia
Level 17/207 Kent Street, Sydney, NSW 2000

First published in 2011
First paperback publication in 2012

ISBN 978 1 40831 186 8 (hardback)
ISBN 978 1 40831 194 3 (paperback)

Text and illustrations © Shoo Rayner 2011

The right of Shoo Rayner to be identified as the author and
illustrator of this work has been asserted by him in accordance
with the Copyright, Designs and Patents Act, 1988.

A CIP catalogue record for this book is available
from the British Library.

1 3 5 7 9 10 8 6 4 2 (hardback)
1 3 5 7 9 10 8 6 4 2 (paperback)

Printed in Great Britain

Orchard Books is a division of Hachette Children's Books,
an Hachette UK company.

www.hachette.co.uk

CHAPTER ONE

Olly gripped his spear tightly and began his run-up. He fixed his gaze on the target: a large prickly bush. Olly pretended it was a huge, hairy boar charging towards him in the forest, grunting and foaming at the mouth with anger.

Olly loved sports like spear-throwing. He lived in Olympia, the town where the Olympic Games were held every four years. He worked at the gym that his dad ran, helping athletes and learning sporting skills from them as they trained. Olly dreamed of being an Olympic champion one day.

As he reached the end of his run-up, Olly let the wooden spear fly from his hand. It arced gracefully through the sky, but it landed quite far from the bush. If it really had been a boar, it would have charged and turned Olly into mincemeat by now!

"That's a good throw!" Eggy cheered. Eggy was the Olympic champion. He was giving Olly some training. The Boys' Throwing Competition was only a few days away, and Olly needed all the help he could get.

"Come on, Spiro, let's see what you can do," Eggy said, smiling.

Spiro worked at the gym with Olly. The two boys were not exactly the best of friends.

Spiro smirked and began his run-up. He hurled his spear into the sky. It wobbled as it flew then shuddered into the ground to the side of the bush.

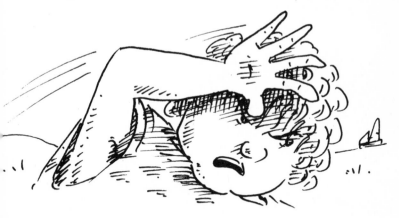

Eggy whistled. "That was a powerful throw, Spiro. Not very accurate, but powerful."

Spiro sneered at Olly. "You'll never be as strong as me!" he chuckled. Then he turned to his dog and pointed at the spear. "Go fetch, boy!"

Spiro's horrible dog, Kerberos, raced off and dragged the spear back to his master.

"It's so unfair," Olly grumbled to himself as he plodded off to retrieve his own spear. "Spiro is a year older than me and he's bigger and stronger. I shouldn't have to compete against him in the Boys' Throwing Competition!"

Kerberos growled a warning as they passed each other on the dusty practice field.

"And I hate that stupid dog of his!" Olly muttered. There was nothing Kerberos enjoyed more than trying to bite large chunks out of Olly's bottom!

The sun shone off Eggy's large, round, bald head. It was the reason he was called Eggy. "Now I'm going to show you how to throw javelins," he said. "They're different to spears. They go much further."

"Yes!" Olly cheered. "That's just what I need in the competition."

Eggy showed the boys how to fit a leather throwing strap around their wrists, and how to hold the loop between their thumb and forefinger. "Now you place the loop into this notch on the javelin," he explained.

"When you throw the javelin," Eggy continued, "the leather loop does all the work. Use the loop to sling the javelin into the sky. Here, watch me."

Eggy took a short run-up and let his javelin fly. He used the loop of leather like a catapult, adding extra momentum to the throw. The javelin landed in the middle of the prickly bush.

"Wow! That's amazing!" Olly cried.

"When you let go, stretch out your throwing arm and point to where you want the javelin to land. Never take your eye off the target until the javelin has landed," Eggy explained.

The javelin was heavier than Olly's own spear. He didn't think he could throw it as far, but he was determined to try.

Olly did exactly as he'd been shown. As he let go of the javelin, he used the loop to add extra power to his throw. The javelin wobbled in the air and landed badly, but it almost reached the bush.

"Brilliant!" Olly whooped. "I've never thrown anything so far before!"

"My turn!" Spiro growled. "I can do better than that!"

But when Spiro let go of his javelin, he didn't sling the loop properly. The javelin's point dropped and stuck in the ground in front of him. Spiro tripped, stumbled and landed in a heap. The javelin clattered on top of his head. "Ow! Stupid thing! Why didn't it go anywhere?"

"Throwing the javelin is an art," Eggy laughed. "It takes talent and lots of practice to get it right. You need to keep working at it right up until the competition starts."

"Huh!" Spiro didn't like to lose at anything. "This is stupid. It's lunchtime!" he growled at Olly, picking up his spear and marching off towards the gym.

"I'd better go. We have to lay the tables for the athletes' lunch," Olly explained to Eggy.

"Well, there's time for a few more practice throws," said Eggy. "Now remember this: let the javelin be part of you. Travel all the way with it in your mind and guide it to where you want it to go. You have to concentrate very hard."

Soon, Olly felt he was getting the hang of it. The javelin flew straight. One time, it landed right next to the bush.

"Well done!" Eggy smiled. "Keep practising and you should do well in the throwing competition."

Olly frowned and looked serious. "I don't want to do well," he said firmly. "I want to win!"

"Ha, ha!" Eggy cheered. "That's what I like to hear!"

CHAPTER TWO

"Hey, Eggy! Catch!" one of the athletes called out, as Eggy walked into the dining room.

Three eggs sailed over the tables. Eggy caught one in each hand, but the third landed squarely on his head and bounced off.

"Lucky they're as hard-boiled as you are, Eggy!" someone else called. Eggy chuckled. It was an old joke and he'd heard it a million times before.

Through all the laughter, Olly and Spiro laid the tables and served bread...

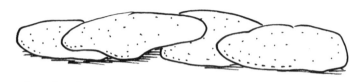

and salads...

and bowls of boiled eggs to the athletes.

Then the room quietened down as Simonedes, the athletes' old, wiry history teacher, climbed up to his podium and cleared his throat.

Every day at lunchtime, Simonedes told the athletes stories about the gods and heroes and all the things they got up to.

It was Olly's favourite time of day. Simonedes was a great storyteller.

"Today I am going to tell you a sad, sad story about Cephalus, the hunter, who had a lovers' tiff with his beautiful wife, Procris.

"Procris ran away from her husband and fled to the forest, where she joined the goddess Artemis, and became a hunter herself.

"But Procris soon realised that Cephalus was the true love of her life and returned home. Cephalus was overjoyed to see Procris again and was very pleased with the gifts she brought him. She gave Cephalus a hound called Laelaps who always caught his prey, and a magic javelin that never missed its target."

"You could do with one of those, Eggy!" someone called out.

The athletes roared with laughter.

Simonedes waited for calm before he went on. "But one fateful day, Procris decided she would follow her husband and see what he got up to when he was hunting in the forest.

"In the dark woods, Cephalus heard a rustling noise coming from some nearby bushes. Thinking it was a wild animal, he picked up his javelin and swiftly hurled it towards the noise. Remember," Simonedes said seriously, "the javelin was magical – it never missed its target."

The room was silent. The athletes waited with baited breath.

"Of course, Cephalus found his beloved wife in the bushes, impaled by the javelin that she had given him. Cephalus never forgave himself. Eventually he threw himself into the sea and drowned, so he could once again be with his one true love."

Sighs filled the room as the athletes pondered poor Procris's fate.

But Olly didn't care about true love. He could only think how wonderful it would be to have a magical javelin that never missed its target. Spiro would never beat him then!

When lunch was over and the tables were cleared, the boys were free for the rest of the day. Olly went looking for Simonedes in the library.

"Could a javelin like that exist?" Olly asked him. "A magic javelin that never misses its target, I mean?"

Simonedes smiled. "Ah yes, it's the Boys' Throwing Competition soon, isn't it? I suppose you're looking for a little special help?" The old man's eyes twinkled. He remembered how much he had wanted to win competitions when he was a boy.

Simonedes thought for a while before he spoke again. "I can tell you that the very first javelin ever thrown was made by the great god Zeus, who is the patron of Olympia and the Olympic Games. You can see him throw his javelins when he sends down lightning bolts from the sky. Those fiery javelins never miss their target!"

Olly's eyes opened wide as he imagined Zeus hurling his javelins of fire from the clouds. "Wow!" he whispered.

"Maybe you should dedicate your javelin to Zeus?" Simonedes smiled. "Carve his name into the wood and maybe Zeus will favour you in the competition!"

CHAPTER THREE

Olly's sister, Chloe, came looking for him a bit later. It was hot and sticky, as if a storm was brewing.

"What are you up to?" Chloe said.

Olly was sitting under a tree in the courtyard, attacking his wooden spear with a sharp piece of flint.

"I'm turning my spear into a javelin for the Boys' Throwing Competition." He showed her how he was carving a notch into the spear. "I found this old strip of leather that I can use as my sling to make the spear go much, much further."

Olly told Chloe all about his javelin lesson with Eggy and about Simonedes' tale of Cephalus and Procris. Then he told her the advice the old man had given him.

"I'm going to make this into a magic javelin that never misses its target, just like the one that Cephalus had. Spiro will never be able to beat me then." Olly sighed happily, imagining himself winning the competition.

A rough voice behind him woke Olly from his daydreams. "Ha, ha! You'll never hit anything on target because you're just a little weakling!"

Spiro had been listening from behind the tree. He grabbed Olly's ear and twisted it nastily. Kerberos narrowed his eyes at Olly and growled threateningly.

"Oh, Kerby-werby! Hello, boy!"
Chloe cooed. Kerberos hated Olly, but
he adored Chloe. His tongue lolled out
of the side of his mouth and he rolled
over at her feet. She tickled his tummy
and he howled with joy.

Spiro let go of Olly to cover his
ears. "Kerberos!" he shouted. "Stop
that horrible noise, now!" He pulled
the dog away from Chloe.

"Magic is the only way you'll ever beat me, Olly!" Spiro jeered, as he ambled off to make trouble somewhere else.

"I hate him!" Olly spat.

"Don't hate him," Chloe soothed. "Just practice and be better than him. You have skill. He's just stupid and has bigger muscles."

"I'll show him," Olly muttered through gritted teeth. "I'll have Zeus on my side!"

CHAPTER FOUR

"This will make my javelin a winner," Olly said to Chloe. "Look, I've carved Zeus's name on it – Simonedes showed me how to write it."

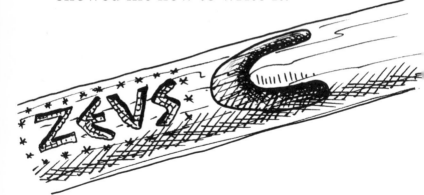

They were at the practice field, where Olly was going to try out his new javelin.

"I hope it works," said Chloe. "Do you think it will?"

Olly just screwed up his eyes and looked at the target. "See that bush over there? I usually pretend it's a giant wild boar."

"It's quite hard to see," said Chloe, screwing up her eyes too. "Those storm clouds are making the sky quite dark."

Olly wrapped the leather thong around his wrist and hooked the loop into the new notch that he had spent hours making.

Olly scratched a throwing line in the dust much further away from the bush than usual. He knew that normally he'd never be able to throw that far, but this time he felt certain he could. He turned and sprang into action.

Reaching the line, he loosed his new javelin and put all his strength and skill into the loop of leather which catapulted it high into the air. Olly held his pose, his gaze fixed on the bush. His throwing arm was steady as a rock, pointing at the target, guiding the missile to its goal.

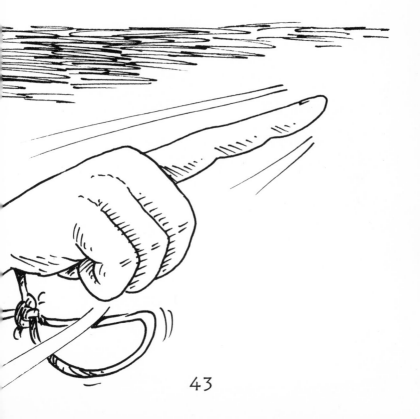

The javelin streaked towards the bush. It landed a few paces to the left of it with a satisfying *thunk!*

"Woah! Did you see that?" Olly cheered. "Spiro will never be able to beat a throw like that."

"Can I have a go?" Chloe said as she ran across the field to fetch the javelin. Chloe had a natural talent for sport, but it was wasted, because girls weren't allowed to take part in games in Olympia. But that didn't stop her having a go when she could!

Olly showed Chloe how to use the leather loop and she fired off a couple of throws. Olly had to admit she was very good at it.

Just then, the air filled with noisy barking. Kerberos ran across the field towards them. Olly hid behind Chloe.

"Keep that dog away from me!" Olly yelled. "He only wants to bite me!"

"You wouldn't bite Olly, would you Kerby, boy?" Chloe cooed.

Kerberos fell at Chloe's feet, a look of joy on his face as she scratched behind his ears.

Spiro came striding across the field. He couldn't believe his luck when he saw Chloe holding Olly's javelin and Olly cowering behind her.

CHAPTER FIVE

"Ha, ha!" Spiro laughed. "Are you practising for the Girls' Throwing Competition, Olly? It's the only competition you've any chance of winning!"

"You'll see, Spiro. I've got a new javelin, and it's going to help me win!" Olly insisted.

"Give it here!" Spiro growled, grabbing the javelin from Olly.

"See that bush?" Olly said. "That's the target. Bet you can't hit it!"

Spiro pushed his face into Olly's. "Watch this."

But Spiro was useless! He kept tangling himself up with the leather loop. He was so desperate to hit the target, he redrew the throwing line closer to the bush four times. Each time Spiro failed, Kerberos fetched the javelin for him.

Patiently, Olly showed Spiro how to use the loop. At last, Spiro threw the javelin in the right direction, almost as far as the bush.

"Ha, ha!" Spiro cheered. "I told you I'm the best. You'll never beat me, Olly. You're just a horrible little…"

Spiro never managed to tell Olly what he was. At that very moment, a loud, low rumble of thunder echoed around the practice ground.

The clouds had turned a dark, liquid grey and the air crackled with electricity. A look of fear spread across Spiro's face. "I've just remembered – erm, I'm meant to be somewhere else," he said, running away with Kerberos yapping at his heels.

"I don't like thunder either," said Chloe, flinching as another clap boomed overhead. She turned to go. "Are you coming, Olly?"

"Zeus won't hurt me. I'm going to keep practising until I hit the target!" Olly said defiantly.

As Chloe ran towards home, Olly wiped Kerberos's spit from his javelin and prepared himself to make his best throw ever.

As thunder crashed all around him, Olly looked up to the turbulent sky and called out to Zeus, the greatest of all the gods.

"Oh, Zeus!" he called, as the wind began to swirl the dust around him. "Let my throw be long and true."

Olly ran up to the throwing line and unleashed his javelin into the wild, stormy air.

The javelin flew straight and true. The dark, leaden sky lit up as Olly's javelin streaked into the heart of the bush. It was instantly followed by an almighty bolt of lightning that crashed to the ground with a deafening explosion. The leaves of the bush flared into a column of fire.

Open-mouthed and stunned, Olly held his throwing pose, pointing at the burning bush, as huge blobs of rain splashed on the dusty ground. "Yaaarooo!" Olly yelled. "Bull's-eye! Dead on target!"

In the middle of the smoking bush, Olly's javelin stood pointing at the sky. Under the carved letters of Zeus's name, a Z-shaped symbol had been burned into the wood by the thunderbolt.

Olly gasped. He raised his head and called into the pouring rain, "Thank you, Zeus. I won't let you down!"

CHAPTER SIX

At the Boys' Throwing Competition a few days later, Eggy examined Olly's javelin. "You've made a good job of this," he said. "It looks amazing. I hope you've learned to throw it just as well?"

"I think I have," Olly smiled, confidently.

"Well, good luck," Eggy said. "Just remember to travel with the javelin in your mind and steer it to the target."

"He'll never throw it that far," Spiro sneered. "Olly's not strong enough, he's just a little weakling."

Olly didn't listen. He watched the other boys throwing at the target, which was a straw model of a wild boar. Olly felt determination surge through him. He was going to hit that target!

Each boy took his turn, and the crowd *ooh-ed* and *ah-ed* as their spear or javelin arced through the air and landed near the target. The boys got points for distance and points for throwing straight, but most attempts fell short and to the side of the target.

Spiro wiped the sweat from his eyes and stormed off to the start of his run-up. His feet hammered the ground as he ran towards the throwing line. With a wail and a grunt, he flung his javelin high into the sky. It wobbled a bit, but it was powerful – too powerful! It sailed right over the target and landed on the other side. It didn't count!

Olly smiled to himself. Sometimes you can be just a bit too strong!

Olly turned and focused on the target in the distance. The crowd hushed as he began his run-up – they seemed to sense something special was about to happen.

At the throwing line, the javelin flew from Olly's hand as if it already knew where to go – as if it was flying under its own magical power.

Olly held his final position, his throwing hand pointing at the exact place where he wanted the javelin to land. In his mind he steered the javelin to the very heart of the target.

It curved towards the ground and pierced the centre of the straw boar, exactly where Olly had planned for it to land.

The crowd erupted in applause as Olly received his olive-leaf crown on the winner's podium.

"That was amazing!" Eggy said. "You'll be the Olympic champion one day or I'll eat my hat!"

As Chloe and his dad hugged him, Olly pressed his fingers firmly into the Z-shaped mark on his javelin.

"Thanks, Zeus!" he whispered.

OLYMPIC FACTS!

DID YOU KNOW...?

The ancient Olympic Games began over 2,700 years ago in Olympia, in southwest Greece.

The ancient Games were held in honour of Zeus, king of the gods, and were staged every four years at Olympia.

Ancient Greek javelins were launched with a leather strap like a catapult, while modern javelins are more like an ancient spear.

There were two events in the ancient Olympic javelin. The aim of one was to hit a target, while the aim of the other was to throw the furthest.

The ancient Olympics inspired the modern Olympic Games, which began in 1896 in Athens, Greece. Today, the modern Olympic Games are still held every four years in a different city around the world.

SHOO RAYNER

RUN LIKE THE WIND	978 1 40831 179 0
WRESTLE TO VICTORY	978 1 40831 180 6
JUMP FOR GLORY	978 1 40831 181 3
THROW FOR GOLD	978 1 40831 182 0
SWIM FOR YOUR LIFE	978 1 40831 183 7
RACE FOR THE STARS	978 1 40831 184 4
ON THE BALL	978 1 40831 185 1
DEADLY TARGET	978 1 40831 186 8

All priced at £8.99

Orchard Books are available
from all good bookshops, or can
be ordered from our website,
www.orchardbooks.co.uk,
or telephone 01235 827702,
or fax 01235 827703.

B51 098 873 3

WITHDRAWN
FROM THE
ROTHERHAM
PUBLIC
LIBRARY

R

This

The
a fu